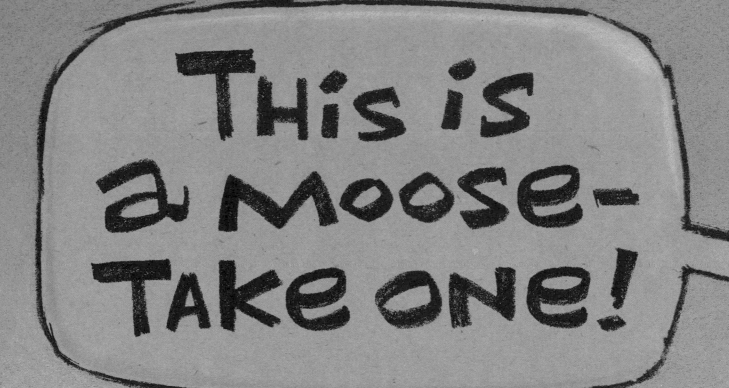

THIS IS A MOOSE

RICHARD T. MORRIS IS AN AUTHOR.

TOM LICHTENHELD IS AN ILLUSTRATOR.

LB

LITTLE, BROWN AND COMPANY

New York Boston

This
is the
Mighty
Moose.

His father
is a moose.

His mother
is a moose.

This moose wants to be an astronaut.

This is a moose - Take Two!
THIS IS A MOOSE
DIR.: BILLY WADDLER
E 2
SCENE: MOOSE INTRODUCTION
CAM.: CHIP N. ZEE

This is the Mighty Moose.

His father
is a moose.

His mother...

Grandmother Moose
and Regal Giraffe

prepare to launch
Mighty Moose into space.

What just happened?

The moose has been launched.

THEY CAN'T DO THAT! THIS IS A FILM ABOUT MOOSE!!

MOOSE→ drinking from lakes.

MOOSE eating leaves.

MOOSE DOING MOOSE THINGS!

Look at that moose go!

But we CAN'T Take Five.
THE MOOSE IS IN OUTER SPACE!
MOOSE IS HERE.
YOU ARE HERE.

I'LL Get Him

Scrappy Squirrel
to the rescue.

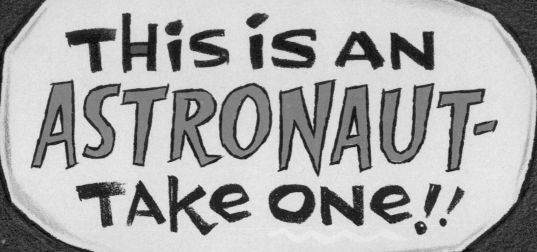

The end

Glossary of Filmmaking Terms

BOOM MICROPHONE: A long pole with a microphone on the end. If you're recording a giraffe, a very long pole is recommended.

CAMERA OPERATOR: A monkey who controls the camera.

CLAPPER: A small board with a hinge that you "clap" to start each take. Watch your paws!

CUT: A term said by the director to end the take. Often used in frustration, as in, "Cut. Cut! *Cut!!!*"

DIRECTOR: A duck in charge of making the movie. Unless, of course, you're filming a moose who wants to be an astronaut.

GAFFER: A bear responsible for lighting the set—always happy to be paid in honey.

MEGAPHONE: A large cone used for making your voice louder. Useful for a director with a moose problem.

ROCKET-POWERED CANOE: *— "Cut!"*

SET: The location where the filming of the movie takes place, either on Earth or on the moon.

TAKE: A single recording of a scene. The more things go wrong, the more takes there are!

For Alice
—*Richard T. Morris*

To my dad, the most influential artist in my life
—*Tom Lichtenheld*

About This Book

This book was edited by Connie Hsu and designed by Tom Lichtenheld and Steve Scott with art direction by Patti Ann Harris. The production was supervised by Erika Schwartz, and the production editor was Christine Ma. This book was printed on 140 gsm Gold Sun Woodfree paper. The type is Stymie and hand-lettering. The illustrations were rendered in ink, colored pencil, and gouache on Mi-Teintes paper, with digital enhancement by Kristen Cella.

Text copyright © 2014 by Richard T. Morris • Illustrations copyright © 2014 by Tom Lichtenheld • All rights reserved. Except as permitted under the U.S. Copyright Act of 1976, no part of this publication may be reproduced, distributed, or transmitted in any form or by any means, or stored in a database or retrieval system, without the prior written permission of the publisher. • Little, Brown and Company • Hachette Book Group • 1290 Avenue of the Americas, New York, NY 10104 • Visit our website at www.lb-kids.com • Little, Brown and Company is a division of Hachette Book Group, Inc. The Little, Brown name and logo are trademarks of Hachette Book Group, Inc. • The publisher is not responsible for websites (or their content) that are not owned by the publisher. • First Edition: May 2014 • Library of Congress Cataloging-in-Publication Data • Morris, Richard T., 1969– • This is a moose / Richard Morris is a writer ; Tom Lichtenheld is an illustrator.—First edition. • pages cm • Summary: Director Billy Waddler is trying to film a documentary about moose, but the moose in question has no intention of spending his life in the woods and his animal friends, who have dreams of their own, help him prove his point. • ISBN 978-0-316-21360-8 • [1. Documentary films—Production and direction—Fiction. 2. Moose—Fiction. 3. Animals—Habits and behavior—Fiction. 4. Humorous stories.] I. Lichtenheld, Tom, illustrator. II. Title. • PZ7.M82862Thi 2014 • [E]—dc23 • 2013015681 • SC • 10 9 8 7 6 5 4 3 • Printed in China

STBY